A SEAL'S VIGILANT HEART

A MIDNIGHT DELTA SERIES NOVELLA, BOOK 7

CAITLYN O'LEARY

PASSIONATELY KIND PUBLISHING INC.

To Those that Have Served, May You Find the Love and Happiness You So Richly Deserve.

SYNOPSIS

A WEDDING: Mason Gault and Sophia Anderson are beyond happy that their wedding day is finally near. Even when Mason comes home injured from a mission, the couple forges ahead knowing their life together is only going to get better.

DREAMS AND DOUBTS: When Sophia is plagued by nightmares that she can't remember in the light of day, and Mason is sure it is because she can't handle the stress of his dangerous job. This hard-headed man will do anything to keep the woman he loves happy, even if it means giving up his dreams.

A RECOMMITMENT: Sophia battles her way through her emotions and finally realizes what is causing her so much anguish. But can she convince her white knight that what she needs is for him to be the man she fell in love with?

1

———

Frannie's head peeked out of the dressing room stall.

"Psst. Sophia. Margie. Get in here." The two women looked at one another in confusion. Frannie was supposed to come out of the dressing room and model her bridesmaid dress on the raised dais in front of all the ladies, just like she had with the last two. Why wasn't she following protocol?

"Just come on out," Lydia Hidalgo encouraged. "We all want to see. The saleslady was sure this one would be perfect."

Frannie's head popped out again. This time, Sophia noted her face was apple red. "Fine, you come in too. Make it quick, before she comes back." The three of them looked at the remaining women, and one girl seated on the couch, shrugged, and then went over to the dressing room with Sophia leading the way. After all, she was the bride-to-be.

Frannie opened the door enough for the three to come in. It was a very tight fit, and that wasn't the only thing fitting tightly. It took all of Sophia's will power not to burst out laughing. Margie wasn't made of such stern stuff. She let out a belly laugh at her best friend's expense.

"Laugh it up, she's out there scoping out dresses with ruffles for you," Frannie said with a glare.

"How in the hell did she get you into that thing? Crisco?" Margie asked, still laughing.

"Just look at my boobs?" Frannie wailed.

"How can I look at anything else?" Lydia asked in awe.

Sophia giggled, then Lydia, and then, so did Frannie. With the corset style dress, her mammoth cleavage started to shake and jiggle, and Sophia feared they were going to be seeing a lot more of their older friend than she would want. Frannie must have realized the potential because she crossed her arms over her bosom.

"Girls, what do I do? She thinks this is the perfect dress for my figure. I don't want to hurt her feelings? What's worse, I don't think I can get out of this dress. I'm going to be stuck wearing it for the next six weeks until the wedding. For God's sake, I'm sixty-five. I knew we should have gone for matching bridesmaid dresses," Frannie wailed.

Out of the corner of her eye, Sophia saw her friend Lydia shudder at the thought.

"Frannie, we couldn't very well have Rebecca wearing the same thing you all would be wearing. She's only fourteen."

"She sure as hell couldn't be wearing whatever this sales woman picks out, she'd end up looking like a streetwalker," Margie warned.

"Not entirely true, you're getting ruffles," Frannie reminded her. "I haven't even shown you girls the worst part."

"It gets worse? How can it get worse?" Margie asked.

Frannie turned around. Margie let out another whoop of laughter. Right across the center of Frannie's ass was a big satin bow.

"Never mind the fact they managed to put a bow on my fattest attribute, how in the hell are you supposed to sit down?"

"You can sit down in this thing? Considering how you're trussed in, it's a wonder you're able to walk."

There was a loud knock.

"Warning. Saleslady coming this way," Ashley Richmond's voice sounded through the opening.

Sophia opened the door, and preceded the others out of the room, just as the sales lady returned with four navy dresses covered in ruffles. Margie was the last one to exit.

"Ms. Daniels, perfect. I can start a room for you. I have some dresses picked out." Frannie choked back a laugh in her dressing room. Ashley grabbed Lydia's arm and pulled Lydia's sister Beth off the couch.

"Ladies, I used to work at a bridal shop," she lied effortlessly to the sales lady, Evelyn. "I have some ideas of what would look great on you for bridesmaid dresses. Let's go hit the racks." She turned to Rebecca, who was the only one still sitting on the couch. "You too, sweetheart."

"Sophia, they're ready for you downstairs for your last wedding gown fitting." Sophia was suffused with a sense of panic.

The saleslady looked over at Ashley. "Do you want me to help?"

"Oh no, you stick with Margie and Frannie, we have this covered," Ashley assured her.

"Hold up." Lydia broke away. "Take Beth and Rebecca, I'm sticking with Sophia," Lydia said. Ashley gave Sophia a once over and nodded at Lydia.

"Sounds like a plan. I'll take Beth and Rebecca; you go with Sophia to her fitting." Before anyone could even blink, Ashley had Beth, and young Rebecca Barnes rushed out of the dressing area. Lydia turned to Sophia.

"Are you okay?"

"I don't know," Sophia answered honestly. "I should be excited, but now I'm scared."

"Of getting married?" Lydia asked gently.

"God no," Sophia said vehemently. "I'd marry Mason tomorrow if possible. No, but what happens if I still don't like the dress? What happens if it doesn't fit right? I can't find a new one now."

"Honey, it's fine. Every woman worries about these things."

"It can't be worse than ruffles," Margie yelled over the top of her dressing room door.

"Or my boobalicious dress," Frannie called out. "Someone rescue me for God's sake, I'm going to need CPR soon."

Everyone, including Evelyn, started to laugh. "Sophia, how about I go down to the fitting area with you," Lydia suggested.

"That would be great." Sophia breathed a sigh of relief.

"Do you know the way?" Evelyn asked.

"Yes." Sophia walked with Lydia.

"Margie and Frannie are crazy, you know that, don't you?" Lydia teased. "I thought I might wet my pants when I saw Frannie in the dress. I've never been around older women who were so much fun. It's great."

"You know, most of the time I don't even think about them being senior citizens," Sophia responded. "They're just my friends. Of course, then they'll refer to my laptop as a typewriter, and I do a double take..." Lydia laughed.

"So tell me more about Ashley," Lydia requested.

"You mean my stepmother?" Sophia said tongue in cheek.

"I wasn't going to go there."

"Then allow me. Ashley is so much better off now she dumped my father. But I worry about her," Sophia said as they reached the bottom of the stairs and turned towards the fitting rooms.

"What do you mean? Why do you worry about her?"

"She's acting out a lot."

"You mean pretending to have sold wedding dresses?"

"Oh no, that's minor. She's been serial dating and almost reverting to teenager behavior. It's like she wants to do everything she can to erase the time she was subjugated by my father."

"How is it impacting your little sister?"

"When she's with her, she's a great mom. But Louisa is spending a lot of time with her grandparents. Dad was such an asshole. He ruined a lot of people's lives."

"There's no way Louisa will end up with your father, will she?"

"God no! Mr. Richmond, Ashley's dad, has Louisa protected every which way. He's amazing.

I'm thankful dad won't have anything to do with raising her."

"From everything you've told me about your father, I agree. I think even though he's Louisa's daddy, she's better off without him."

"Billy and I would have been better off without him, that's for sure," Sophia said. She suddenly smiled. "Lydia, it's the first time I said it without being bitter. I think I've finally put the past in the past. God, I love Mason."

"What does Mason have to do with it?" Lydia was confused with the abrupt change of topic.

"He's helped me so much to get past my bitterness. He's helped me, in so many ways."

"Boy, do I hear that. Those SEAL boys are amazing. Don't tell Clint, because I don't want him to get a swelled head, but he's been my rock." Lydia's expression was dreamy as she thought about her fiancé, Clint Archer.

"We are pretty lucky, aren't we?"

"We are." Lydia gave Sophia a hug.

"Hello? Are you Sophia Anderson?" A woman with a thick German accent asked.

"Yes, that's me."

"I'm Betta, and I have your dress ready to try on."

The woman held open the curtain to the dressing room, and Sophia went inside. Lydia gave her a wink and a thumbs-up.

Betta helped Sophia into the dress, but it wasn't until she was totally cinched in that she was allowed to turn around and look in the mirror. She gasped. The lace and beaded corset bared her shoulders and flowed into a silk skirt.

"What? Are you all right, Sophia?" Lydia asked from outside the room. "Can I come in?"

Betta opened the curtain.

"Oh my. Oh my. Sophia, you look stunning. There couldn't be a dress any more perfect for you. You look like a glamorous movie star from a bygone era."

Sophia bit her thumb. *Was that a good thing?*

"You look like a fucking pin-up girl. Mason is going to lose his shit," Ashley said. "My God, who in the hell helped pick this out? They should have earned a double commission."

"Where did you come from?" Lydia asked.

"The saleslady made us come downstairs when Ashley tried to help one of her other customers," Rebecca said as she giggled.

Sophia smiled at the woman who ended up becoming a good friend, despite the fact she'd had the bad sense to marry Sophia's father.

"Margie and Frannie came with me to pick out the dress," Sophia told Ashley in answer to her question.

"I knew I liked them," Ashley said with a bright smile.

"Oh my God, can they come help pick out my dress?" Beth asked.

"Your bridesmaid dress?" Sophia asked in confusion. "But I like the one you're wearing." She looked at the three different styles of navy dresses each girl was wearing and they each looked great.

"No, not the bridesmaid dress. My wedding dress. I would love to look half as good as you." Sophia looked at the beautiful Hispanic girl in disbelief. Before she could protest, Lydia gave her 'the hand', demanding her silence.

"Beth's right. You look too good for words, Sophia. I can't wait to see Mason's face when you walk down the aisle."

Sophia looked in the mirror. Really looked at herself, and finally breathed a sigh of satisfaction. She *did* look good.

"You really do, Sophia," Rebecca agreed shyly.

Sophia blushed when she realized she'd spoken her thoughts out loud. She smoothed her hands over the mermaid-style satin dress and grinned. Lydia came up from behind her and gave her a hug. She whispered in her ear. "That SEAL won't know what hit him."

Sophia looked at her wedding dress and an overwhelming wave of sadness washed over her. It hit her from out of the clear blue sky. Her mother should have been here for this. As a child, she used to draw pictures of wedding dresses and show her mother. It had been a fun thing between the two of them, and now her mom wasn't here to see the dress she had actually chosen. *Why aren't you here, Mom?*

"Oh Sophia, they did a marvelous job," Frannie's voice boomed throughout the downstairs area. Sophia saw Frannie and Margie come up behind her in the mirror and was delighted to see they were in stylish dresses that flattered their respective figures.

"Why did they send you downstairs? Were you misbehaving too?" Ashley asked.

"Frannie always misbehaves," Margie answered. "But this time, we demanded to see Sophia. We wanted to see her final fitting. You look gorgeous, Sophia."

"Margie, get me a tissue. I'm going to cry." Margie found a fast food napkin in her purse and handed it to Frannie.

"All of you look so beautiful. This wedding is going to be spectacular," Margie said with a wide smile.

"She's right. Rebecca, you look lovely," Sophia enthused. "Billy won't know what hit him."

"Really? Are you sure this is within the budget? It seems like a lot." The girl eyed the price tag on her dress.

Five voices rang out assuring her the dress was well within the budget of the wedding, and Sophia loved her friends for it. Rebecca was a foster child and always worried about things, even though she now had a foster mother who would easily purchase the dress for her. Rebecca was still very conscientious about money.

"Okay, now that I have burned two thousand calories doing contortions to get in and out of dresses, who's up for lunch? I vote for Mexican food. I desperately need a margarita," Frannie called out.

A round of 'yes's' sealed the deal.

Sophia took one last look in the mirror and gave a secret smile. *Yes, Mason is going to love seeing me in this dress.*

2

IF HE WAS TOLD ONE MORE FUCKING TIME IT WAS A quick in and out mission, he was going to quit the SEAL team! Lieutenant Mason Gault gripped his Sig Sauer P239 and glanced at Drake Avery out of the corner of his eye. His second in command was angry, but he really didn't give a shit. He was in command, and if someone was going to take the risk on this goat fuck, it was going to be him.

Mason didn't mind hard assignments, hell he relished *impossible* assignments. That's what he and his team were trained for, the reason they had signed up to be SEALs. But this was the third time in a row the intelligence had been one hundred percent wrong. Thank God his gut had warned him, and he and his team had double-timed it to the Middle Eastern village where the reporters were being held.

Supposedly they were going to be ransomed, and it was Mason's team's job to rescue them. However, when they got there, the city square was filled for public beheadings. It was clear by the faces of the people many of them were too scared not to attend, and the armed guards around the perimeter had forced them to be there.

Mason, Drake, Finn, Clint, Jack, and Aiden had scouted the area for the last twenty minutes. Aiden was going climb to one of the high points and act as a sharp shooter if necessary. They were hoping it wouldn't be. If it came to that, they were toast, since the odds were easily five to one and they still had to get three civilians the hell out of Dodge. He was also going to be the eyes of the team, and *that* was definitely needed.

Clint was going to be the one coordinating communications again. Every one of the men was wearing a tracking device so he would know their whereabouts. As soon as one of them got ahold of the civilians, they would be tagged with trackers as well. It was Clint's job to coordinate with Aiden to come up with the best escape route and to stay on the ass of their extraction team.

Finn had already provided Mason, Drake, Jack and himself with thaubs, the Arabic robes would disguise their fatigues and vests. However, in this village only about twenty percent of the men wore them, so there was still a chance they would stand out. Thank God Finn also scored agals to wear on their heads. Otherwise, Jack with his blond hair would stick out like a sore thumb.

The scaffolding where the executions were to take place looked brand new, which to Mason's way of thinking was a very good sign. It meant this was the first time the terrorists had performed a high-profile execution in this village, so they weren't practiced. Drake, Jack, and Finn were to mingle with the crowd while Mason went to the building behind the scaffolding where they had to be holding the reporters. It's what had Drake's panties in a twist.

"We should all go," Drake hissed as he got in his face.

"Okay guys, spread out. We need coverage, and you know it. We'll be connected via radio," Mason said pointing to the barely seen transmitter in his ear and the mic somewhat covered by the headdress.

"That's bullshit, Mase. You should, at least, take one more man to where we think the hostages are. We're not lone rangers. We're a team."

"I fucking know that, Drake. But if I'm too late, or I don't make it, then I'm going to need you guys to get them before they walk up the stairs to the platform. That's going to require the three of you, and you know it." Drake gave him a hard stare and finally nodded.

Mason went first around the corner and mingled with the crowd. He knew the others would follow. Clint was set up in the falling down building, and Aiden should be in place by the time Mason made it to his target.

The crowd was thick with people. He couldn't believe the number of women and children who had been made to come and watch this spectacle. The kids had picked up on their parent's discomfort and were crying. He got closer to one of the sentries and saw he was basically a kid. When he looked closer, he saw the muzzle of his rifle was bent. There was no way he was going to be a threat.

"Check out the sentries," he whispered quietly into his mic. "The guy closest to me has a weapon that won't fire. We might be in for some luck."

"Roger that," Finn said.

"Gotchya," Drake answered. "Checking now."

"Yes, Sir," Jack said. He was still new to the team and pretty deferential. Mason knew it would change quickly.

"Count 'em off and give me their positions. I'll coordinate with Aiden," Clint said.

Mason provided info on the guards he passed as he made his way to the building where they hoped the reporters were located. He heard as, at least, seven more were identified with inoperable rifles, and he reported two more. Mason did a mental fist pump.

He couldn't believe it when he got to the building, and there wasn't a single guard posted at the side entrance. The intel had been right about one thing, they were dealing with amateurs. He pushed the door in slightly, holding his gun to the side.

A man pulled the door open with a frown and got out two words in Arabic before going for the rifle he had propped up against the wall. Mason rushed him, and using his K-Bar knife took care of him with one well-placed cut. Yelling came from someplace on the second floor. He reached the bottom of the stairs, peeked around, but didn't see anyone.

As quickly as he could, Mason did an entire check of the bottom floor and found only one other lackadaisical guard who he was easily able to subdue. There were no other ways down to the bottom floor, which was perfect since the entrance to the public square was on the main floor of the building. He hit his mic.

"Clint."

"Here, boss."

"Anyone who's close, converge on me, ASAP. We have a good shot at an ambush."

"Hall-a-fucking-lujah."

The yelling continued, and then Mason heard a high pitched scream from the second floor. It took everything he had not to rush upstairs. He knew one of the reporters was being tortured. A sliver of light shone as Drake pushed open the side door. He moved like a ghost to plant himself beside Mason.

Another shrill scream sounded.

Another sliver of light as Jack entered the building. It was enough. Mason lifted his fist and pointed up the stairs. He went first. They were careful, and did everything by the book, not knowing what was waiting for them.

Two screams. Two different voices. Yelling in Arabic and laughter, then Mason could hear the clear sound of electricity. Fuckers were probably using cattle prods. They got to the top of the stairs and walked into a horror house of torture. One man was hanging from a meat hook, naked. He was unconscious. The two others were tied to chairs with hoods over their heads, and seven men with long cattle prods circled around them randomly zapping them.

In a moment, Mason saw their rifles were either on the floor or against the walls, and their side arms were holstered.

He knew his men realized the same thing. All three knew they weren't to take any shots, just make sure these seven men were dead as quick as possible and then get the reporters the fuck out of this hell hole.

The fight was over in less than a minute. Mason barely felt the knife wound from the man behind him. He'd have to assess it after they got out of the building, right now it wasn't something to slow him down.

"You're cut." Mason wasn't surprised to see Finn coming up the stairs with his arms full of additional robes. Jack was cutting down the reporter, and Drake had finished untying one of the reporters who was sobbing.

"Sir, I'm Chief Petty Officer Drake Avery, one of the Navy SEALs, who's been sent to rescue you. I need you to calm down." Drake's soothing tone seemed to be getting through to the man. He gripped Drake's arms.

"I'm Dick Lloyd, do you think you can really get us out of here alive?"

"Absolutely."

And they would. It's what they did.

"Mason." He turned to Finn. "I have some men who are going to help us. They are some of the villagers who were forced to attend the beheading. They have the downstairs covered."

God Bless Finn Crandall and his scavenging and language abilities. Mason knew you could send Finn into a Men's dormitory, and he'd manage to find a beauty queen, clown, and a proctologist.

"Finn, how many men do we have downstairs to help us?"

"Three. Five counting the ones driving the trucks."

"What trucks?"

"The trucks I hotwired. Since these assholes were in here with the reporters, and the rest of them were out front guarding their citizens, I hotwired two trucks so we could make our escape. I figured we could use some drivers, so I found some help." Mason grinned and patted Finn on the shoulder then he hissed in pain.

"Mase let me take a look at that, you're dripping blood." Finn moved the robe off of Mason's shoulder.

"Later, let's get them loaded up." He looked around, his team had already gotten the reporters into the robes. He pressed his communication device. "Did you get all of that Clint?"

"Got it. Aiden's coming down to where I am. We don't have robes. Will you be able to come and pick us up?"

"Affirmative," Mason responded. "Sit tight."

Drake, Finn, and Jack worked with Dick Johnson to hustle the other two reporters downstairs and into the two waiting trucks.

Finn talked to the villagers, in each truck one of them would sit up front while Finn and Drake rode shotgun. They circled the crowd and soon had picked up Clint and Aiden.

"Transport is waiting for us. With our sweet rides, it should take us less than an hour," Clint reported.

"Let me see your wound," Clint demanded in the back of the truck. Mason had already forgotten about it in the heat of the mission, but now Clint had mentioned it, the knife wound began to throb.

"God dammit, I don't want to be injured right before my fucking wedding," Mason bitched.

"Too late. So let's, at least, minimize the damage. Hold still and let me bandage it." Clint pulled out makeshift supplies. Mason winced as his friend worked on his wound and the truck bounced.

"This isn't fucking fair. Darius had to be AWOL for this mission because he needed additional fucking medical training. I get injured, and I'm stuck with you?" Clint laughed and so did Aiden.

"If it had been life threatening, I would have worked on you, Lieutenant," Aiden assured him.

"I see the size of your hands, you probably would have killed me with your deft touch," Mason groused. Again the men laughed at him, but all the talking helped keep his mind off the pain.

"All done. You're going to need some stitches–"

"A lot of stitches," Aiden interrupted.

"But it didn't hit any tendons or ligaments just meat," Clint continued.

"You did a good job," the Senior Chief said to Clint. "Lieutenant, your entire team is top notch. This operation went slick as snot. After the shitty intel, we received I didn't think it was possible."

Mason looked at the man who was ten years his senior. He might outrank him, but everyone knew a Senior Chief Petty Officer was go-to guy after the Lieutenant and was often more respected. This was the second mission Aiden had assisted Midnight Delta with, and Mason was strongly considering asking him to stay on in a permanent capacity.

"Thanks for the kind words, Aiden."

"Just telling the truth as I see it. You have a strong team, and you do a great job leading them."

"Damn right he does. Wait until you see him at headquarters tearing it apart about the faulty intel. He'll do it respectfully of course," Clint said tongue-in-cheek.

Mason and Aiden laughed.

The truck stopped. They heard the sound of incoming helicopters.

"Gentlemen, our ride is here," Clint said.

"Thank fuck." Mason grinned. "I have a bride to get home to."

"I'LL BE at the house by tonight, honey." Sophia gripped her cell phone and thought her face might crack in half because of her grin.

"Oh God, this seemed like the longest time ever. I'm sending Billy over to Todd's house for a sleepover."

"I think that sounds like a great idea." Sophia heard talking in the background. "I've got to go. I should see you before midnight."

"I'll be waiting. I love you."

"I love you too, Sophia." She traced her finger over Mason's picture on her phone, and then pressed on the speed dial for the diner.

"Margie?"

"Yes."

"It's Sophia, I won't be coming into work tomorrow."

"Well hot damn, your boy must be back in town."

"He just called." Sophia let out a relieved laugh.

"Well give Frannie a call. You know she likes to be told immediately."

"Right after I text Billy." Sophia smiled.

"Good girl."

Sophia pressed end and then sent a text to Billy. He didn't answer, but she knew he would see it between classes. She was so relieved Mason was on his way home. In the two years they'd been together, he'd been on countless missions, but she worried every time and knew Billy did too. Next, she pressed in the number for Frannie DeLuca.

"Hey Sophia, please tell me you're not calling to go dress shopping."

"Nope, I'm calling to let you know Mason is coming home! He'll be here tonight."

"That's great news. Do you need anything? I can bring over some food if you don't feel like cooking."

"Nope, I'm just going to clean up."

"What are you talking about? The house is spotless. I bet you make your bed every morning." Sophia winced. Was she that obvious?

"Well, I have to change the sheets. Plus I want to bake some of his favorite things. I appreciate your offer, but I want to cook for him. It makes me feel good. I'll get it done before he gets home."

"So you both can do the important 'cooking.' I get it. I might be old, but I have my Tony. So don't think I don't know what you're going to be doing on those clean sheets."

"Frannie, how do I always end up in these types of conversations with you and Margie?"

"Because you don't have your Mama to have these conversations," Frannie said gently. She was right. What's more, it was something that had been plaguing Sophia since the wedding planning went into full swing.

"How did you know?" she asked quietly.

"Oh baby girl. You're never too old to miss your Mama. I still miss mine, and I'm sixty-five."

"But Billy seems to have gotten over it. He hardly ever talks about our mom anymore."

"Of course, he doesn't," Frannie answered. "He has you. Your mom was sick for a long time. You practically raised that boy. Biologically you might be his sister, but you're the mother of his heart." Frannie's words resonated with her. When she thought how much her opinion of Rebecca mattered to Billy, she realized he had treated her like a beloved parent.

"Frannie, I'm not sure I'm up to that level of responsibility. Sure, Mason and I are talking about starting a family, but I worry I don't have what it takes to be a good mother."

Sophia pulled the phone from her ear at her friend's loud laughter. As Frannie settled down, she finally got words out.

"You've got to be kidding me. You're one of the most nurturing people I know, Sophia Anderson soon-to-be Gault. You're going to be a fantastic mother. Billy thinks the sun rises and sets with you." Sophia's cheeks heated.

"Frannie, I–"

"I think you should start working on making babies immediately. Get rid of the rubbers."

"Frannie!"

"Okay, if not the rubbers throw away the pills. I want to be holding your son or daughter by next year."

"You're outrageous."

"You're just figuring it out now?" Sophia laughed some more. Nope, she'd known for quite some time that Frannie DeLuca was outrageous, and it was why she loved her so much. She also knew the woman was trying to lift her spirits, and she greatly appreciated it.

"Sophia, are you still there?"

"I'm here. Have I told you how much I love you?"

"Ah, I love you too. Both Tony and I love you like you were our own. Now hurry up and give us a beautiful baby to love on."

"We will, we will. First, I have to change the sheets."

"Clean sheets are not a prerequisite. I thought they explained things better than that in health class."

"Good-bye, Frannie."

"Good-bye, Sophia."

Sophia hung up the phone with a smile. She always ended up smiling after talking to Frannie. She had really been gifted with some great people in her life, but none was better than Mason Gault. She still thought about that night in the alley when he rescued her from her attackers. She rubbed at the scar on her arm. He'd saved her twice, once from the initial attack, and then after she'd been kidnapped. He truly was her knight in shining armor, and now she was going to get to marry him. A smile blossomed on her face, and she pressed her palms against her cheeks. Life didn't get much better than this.

3

MASON WAS NERVOUS, AND HE WAS *NEVER* NERVOUS. Of course, this was the first time he'd come home wounded.

He shut off the radio as he exited the Five Freeway, and took the side streets that led him to the home he shared with Sophia and Billy. His shoulder throbbed, and it pissed him off. He loved it when she launched herself into his arms, and he carried her into their bedroom. If he did it tonight, he'd probably tear the stitches. Dammit! He'd have to tell her about the injury right from the get-go. He hit the steering wheel hard.

"Fuck!" That had hurt. He had to remember not to use his right hand for a few days.

He had no idea how she was going to take it. They never really had a deep dark discussion about the dangers of his job. Sophia seemed to take it in stride, and that was enough for him. What happened if this changed things?

Fuck. Are my palms actually wet?

He and the guys always said they would only want to be with women who understood their need to be SEALs. Their need to serve their country and the fact it included going on dangerous missions. He always assumed Sophia was that kind of woman because she had handled it so well when he left in the past. But what if this injury changed things? Mason couldn't imagine a life not leading his SEAL team. But he couldn't imagine a life without Sophia either.

This time, he used his left hand to massage the tense muscles in the back of his neck.

He made the last turn down the street to their house and pulled into the driveway. The door flew open, and there she was. All of his worries temporarily flew out of his mind as he looked at the breathtaking woman who had agreed to marry him. She was wearing a yellow sundress that looked beautiful in the moonlight. She waited for him on the top stair of the side door at the kitchen, ready for the launch. Mason was slow getting out of his truck. He didn't bother with his duffle; he'd get it in the morning. Sophia was practically vibrating with excitement and he grinned at her. But her smile dimmed as he walked slowly around the cab of the truck.

"Mason?" His name was a question.

"I'm all right."

She moved faster than he had ever seen. In less time than it took to blink she was in front of him, looking up at him, her hands on his chest, and then cupping his cheeks.

"Mason, what happened? Should you have been driving? Do you need help getting inside?" He looked at her in amazement. There was no wailing, no censure, no histrionics, nope, nothing.

"I need a kiss. I need my welcome home kiss. I'm only sorry I won't be able to carry you to our bedroom."

He watched as she bit her lip. "I think I need our kiss more than I ever have before," she said.

She stood on tiptoe, and he scooped her up with both arms, uncaring about the pain in his right shoulder. He needed to feel Sophia pressed against him. He was hungry for the taste of her, and he ravished instead of seduced. She trembled and forced himself to pull away.

"Too much?"

"Not enough. It's never enough but tonight it's worse." Her green eyes were shiny, and it wasn't just the reflection of the moon.

"I'm safe. I came back to you. I'll always come back to you."

Her head dipped down for a moment, and then she looked back at him. "I love you. And I need you, handsome." She gave him a saucy grin. "And, since you can't carry me does it mean I get to finally carry you?" Mason shouted with laughter.

"How about we race to the bedroom?" Sophia shot him a worried glance.

"It's my shoulder, honey. I can race just fine. I'll need some help getting out of my clothes. Are you willing to play nursemaid?"

"Who's been helping you when I wasn't around? Drake? I swear that man has had a secret crush on you for years."

"Nah, it was Clint. You're going to have to break it to Lydia that he's probably going to end up leaving her because of his unrequited love for me." He threw his arm around Sophia, glad she was willing to banter instead of obsessing about his injury. He'd been worried about nothing. Now he could focus on the important thing—making love to the woman who owned his heart.

When they were finally naked on their bed, she kissed him on top of the large bandage on his shoulder.

"How many stitches, Mason?"

"About the same amount you had when you were attacked."

"Then should we be doing this? You could end

up pulling them out. Maybe you need to rest." He was kneeling in front of her. He pulled her hand to the front of his thighs so she could caress his throbbing cock.

"I would end up far more injured if I weren't allowed to make love to you tonight. You're my compass. Anytime I get lost or something goes wrong all I have to do is think about my Sophia, and I know where I am supposed to be. My place is with you."

Mason cupped her cheek.

"Tonight I need to touch you."

He kissed the side of her lips.

"I need to kiss you."

He stroked downwards until he was cupping her breast, his thumb lazily brushed forays around her nipple.

"I need to caress you."

Mason smiled as Sophia moaned in pleasure. Then he groaned, as she shifted her hand and began to stroke up and down, measuring his need.

"I need to caress you too, Mason."

She bent forward and licked one flat nipple, and he shuddered in response.

"I need to kiss you."

He pulled her hand away from his erection, knowing he wouldn't last if she continued to caress him. He drew both of her arms up so they twined around his neck, and gave her the kiss they both needed. A butterfly soft brush of lips, teasing and tantalizing until they both opened and sighed. The kiss morphed into a languid play of tongues, seducing and loving. For long minutes they pressed closer and closer together, their mouths gently gliding in a passionate mating confirming they were once again back together.

Sophia whimpered, and Mason tasted salt.

"Baby, what is it? What's wrong?"

"It's too much." Her nails bit into his neck, and her nipples were pebbled against his chest. He'd been so intent on not rushing her, on holding back his own passion so she could have the time and gentleness he thought she needed, that he hadn't realized she was as hungry as he was.

Mason eased her down onto their bed. His fingers slid into the silk of her hair, spreading it across the pillow, loving the way the golden strands contrasted against the blue colored cotton. She grasped his short hair so he was forced to look at her.

"Play later, I need you now," she said in a voice hoarse with want. In all of their time together, he'd never seen this level of intensity.

"Sophia?"

"I could have lost you," her voice broke, and her eyes slammed shut. She bit her lip and swallowed. When she opened them again, they were bright with unshed tears. "Please don't make me beg, Mason."

"Never, baby. Never." He shifted, and found a welcome between her already spread thighs. "I need this as badly as you do." He began the slow slide into her body, she was soft, silky, and responsive. It felt like he was truly coming home.

"So good," she murmured as she lifted her knees and clutched him. "All the way Mason, don't hold back."

Finally, they were as close as two people could be, and he groaned with satisfaction. "You're perfect, Sophia."

"You're my Mason. My white knight. You're the one who's perfect." His heart went into overdrive. He wanted to be that for her. He needed to be that for her. Then all higher thought went out the window as she clenched around him.

"Again, baby. Do it again." She gave him a sultry smile.

He pushed in, and she cried out, her neck arched as she clenched again. They continued the dance, pleasuring one another, higher and higher.

"More, Mason," she gasped. He lowered his head and licked her nipple. She began to pant. She raised her legs and locked her ankles around his hips. He began the final drive, taking them upwards.

He looked into the emerald depths of her eyes

and saw his past, his future, his forever and knew no matter what, she was the only thing in the world that truly mattered.

"I love you, Sophia," he cried. They crashed into heaven together.

———

LYING IN MASON'S ARMS, having him stroke her hair was almost, *almost*, as good as making love with him. She pressed her ear against his chest and listened to the beat of his heart.

"So what did you do while I was gone?"

"I–" His stomach rumbled loudly, and she peeked at him through her lashes.

"Ignore it, I want to hear about the last ten days."

"I have lasagna warming in the oven."

"We'll eat later. I've missed you. I want to hear every detail of how you spent your time. I know you were planning on some girl time with Rebecca, did you get to do that?" She loved he remembered what she had told him and was genuinely interested in her life.

"We went out to–"

His stomach growled even louder.

"Did I tell you I have vanilla ice cream and homemade brownies for dessert?" He pushed her off his chest, and she went sprawling in a heap of giggles.

"To hell with the lasagna, I'm having dessert first, then dinner, then dessert again." He gave her butt a swat, and she laughed even harder.

She stayed in bed and enjoyed the view as he pulled on a pair of jeans. God, the man had the best ass in the entire Universe. She was going to have to take a bite when they got back in bed. He looked at her over his shoulder.

"Quit ogling and come into the kitchen with me. I don't want to eat alone. I've missed you too much."

Her heart melted. She got out of bed and pulled on the shirt he had been wearing. She loved wearing his shirts. She had worn one every night while he was gone. He grabbed her hand, and they walked to the kitchen.

"Milk or ice cream with your brownies?" she asked.

He was right behind her with his chin propped on her shoulder. "What are you having?"

"Milk."

"Then I'll have milk to begin with. I'll have a brownie sundae after dinner."

"Well, you'll be eating that by yourself."

"I bet I can tempt you into taking a bite." He probably could. He was very good at tempting her into things.

She got the milk, and he got the glasses. When she went to sit down, he coaxed her into sitting on his lap.

"God Sophia, you are the world's best baker. How is the business going? How's the diner?"

"Busy," she said with a deep sigh. "I'm still bummed about Irene quitting. She was doing so well. But this new girl Corrine is getting the hang of things quickly. I already gave her a small raise so she would be incented to stay."

"Can you afford it?" He broke off a piece of his brownie and offered it to her. She stared into his deep blue eyes, took the milk chocolate treat, and then sucked his fingers into her mouth.

"Sophia," he breathed.

"Yes. Yes, I can."

"What?" he asked in a dazed voice.

"Yes, I can afford to give her a raise." She smiled.

"Good God woman, how can you multi-task like that? You start in with that licking thing, and I can't keep up with a conversation. So things are going that well with the business?"

"Mason, I had to turn down two stores because I wouldn't be able to keep up the level of service and quality people have come to expect. They said they would up the amount they'd be willing to pay, and they'll wait for us. One of the store owners asked to have lunch with me. She is part of a

Women in Business Network she'd like me to join."
Sophia still couldn't believe it. She never would
have thought of herself as a businesswoman.

"That's great, honey."

The brownies were gone. She got up to get the
lasagna out of the oven.

As they ate their meal, Sophia regaled Mason
with Frannie's bridesmaid dress debacle.

"I don't understand. The dresses aren't going to
match?" he asked as he scooped his third helping
of pasta.

"No, they're all navy colored, but the styles will
be different to flatter the figure of the woman or girl
wearing it. What will look good on Ashley won't
necessarily look appropriate for Rebecca."

"Makes sense. So tell me what your dress looks
like," Mason asked innocently.

"Oh, I got a red one. It's really pretty. It'll look
great for our wedding photos. I especially like the
sequins."

"There was a time, Miss Anderson when you
weren't such a smart ass." Mason grinned at her.

"It must be the company I keep. If you're a good
boy, after your dessert you'll get an even better
dessert. But if you keep asking sneaky questions I
might be too tired."

"You've convinced me, no more sneaky
questions. Stay put and I'll clean up and get the ice
cream." He brushed a kiss on the top of her head as

he cleared the table. She saw him wince as he used his right hand but she chose to ignore it. Tonight was a celebration. This was a time for them to enjoy the moment not for her to focus on what might have been.

4

"So what's wrong?"

"Nothing's wrong?" Mason was thoroughly sick of this line of questioning. Drake had been at it for ten minutes, and he could have stopped eight minutes ago as far as he was concerned.

"Would you back off already?" Clint bent to pick up one of the basketballs and place it on the rack at the side of the court. "Let the man be, he just got his stitches out and finally got to really exercise. Maybe he's feeling his age."

"No, that's not it," Drake said eyeing Mason thoughtfully. "He's been off for a week now. He hasn't acted all commander-ish."

"Well, I am now Avery. Shut the fuck up. There is nothing wrong." Mason winced. He didn't sound authoritative, he sounded desperate.

"Ah-Ha. I knew it. Spill it."

"Maybe I'm just upset Finn missed the last basket," Mason said glancing over at his teammate. Finn shook his head.

"Don't try and blame me. I'm with Drake. I wasn't going to call you on it. But now you're dragging my name through the mud..."

"Okay, it's the girl's bachelorette party," Mason lied. "I'm worried. Lydia was supposed to be the one planning it since she's the maid of honor, but Ashley has taken over, and she's scary."

Darius did a double take.

"Ashley? And Sophia is going for it?"

"I actually think Sophia is kind of excited. Even when she went to the community college, she was kind of sheltered because she had to go home most nights to take care of her mother."

"Lord save us," Drake said. They headed out of the gymnasium into the bright California sunshine. "Why isn't she doing like you are and having a PG bachelorette party since Rebecca is one of the bridesmaids."

"Because they're having a bridal shower and that will include Rebecca. The bachelorette party is for the adults, and like I said, Ashley took over," Mason groaned. The more he talked about it, the more he realized he was concerned. But not as concerned as he *was* about Sophia's trouble sleeping. Still, this wasn't something he felt comfortable talking about with the guys.

"I think I have an idea," Drake said.

"God save us," Darius groaned.

"Seriously, Drake, you don't need to help," Mason backpedaled. The last thing he needed was Drake Avery to insert himself.

"No seriously, it's a good plan."

"Okay, tell us," Finn prodded.

"It's still in its infancy. Let me do a little bit more planning."

"Oh God, save us," Finn groaned.

"Here, here," Darius seconded. Mason clasped his head in his hands. This did not bode well.

SOPHIA, Beth, and Lydia were still slightly stunned as they sat in Ashley's bedroom. She had moved out of the home she had shared with Sophia's father. Now she was living in a gated community in a ritzy suburb of San Diego not far from her parent's home. What had the three women so amazed was the built-in lit make-up area that looked like something you would see backstage in a theater dressing room. Currently, Ashley was applying her make-up.

"Close your mouths, girls. Beth, you're next."

"I couldn't possibly."

"Not only am I doing your make-up but I've also picked outfits for each of you."

"I'm happy with what I'm wearing," Lydia said decisively. "And there isn't a chance in hell you're doing my make-up."

"Lydia, I love you to pieces, but hon, you only have on eyeliner, lipstick, and mascara. I've never seen you wear anything else. Do you even know how to apply more makeup?" Sophia watched as Lydia squirmed.

"Seriously, girls. Don't you want to learn how to apply makeup?"

"I would," Beth said shyly.

"That's why you're next."

"I'm satisfied with what I have." Lydia was resolute.

"Fine. But I've arranged for someone to come in to do hair and make-up for Sophia's wedding. Frannie and Margie are thrilled, and you'll have to suck it up."

"I–" Lydia started to protest.

"That better be the sound of you sucking," Ashley said.

"That's gross." Sophia felt like she was watching a tennis game between two evenly matched players.

"Lydia, are you trying to tell me my makeup doesn't look good?" Ashley demanded.

Sophia knew her friend had won. "No," was Lydia's soft reply. Ashley took out some wipes and cleaned her face.

"Voila, a blank canvass. This is really simple, and it doesn't take much."

Sophia went over to watch, with Beth and Lydia following. Ashley was right, she really didn't apply a lot, and the transformation was subtle but amazing. She got up and pushed Beth into the chair. Soon Beth's big black eyes were even bigger and sparkled like gems.

"Lydia?"

"Okay. But I'm not changing outfits."

In the end, all four girls were wearing cute dresses from Ashley's closet, their eyes sparkled, and their lips were plump and shiny.

"Now we are going to the cutest little place for dinner. It's in the Gaslamp Quarter, and the waiters are big ole flirts. They pour the best martinis. You'll love it."

"I'm not drinking I'm the designated driver," Lydia said.

"Girl, you're getting on my last nerve." Ashley rolled her eyes. "I have you covered. I've arranged for a limo tonight. He's even going to drive you home. He has a partner who will drive your car home behind us. It's all good."

Sophia was amazed. To think this girl had been under her father's thumb and afraid to leave him. As if she read her mind, Ashley looked at her and winked.

"I've definitely come into my own. Tonight I intend to really enjoy myself."

"Well, I draw the line at a strip club."

"Eww. I don't want some man wagging his thing at me in public either," Ashley said. Sophia breathed a sigh of relief. "We are however going to a bar I know where they have karaoke and dancing."

"I don't sing," Lydia said.

"That's not true. Now you're being stubborn. You need to pull the stick out of your butt," Beth said to her sister. Sophia and Ashley laughed. Sophia never would have expected Beth to have said that to her sister.

"Okay, maybe I do sing," Lydia relented. "But I'm going to need one or two of those martinis."

Ashley's phone beeped. "The limo is here. Let's get a move on."

"Give me your phone," Sophia requested. "I want to see pictures of Louisa." Ashley handed over the phone as they headed downstairs. Sophia thumbed through the pictures.

"I can't believe how big she's getting."

"She's beautiful like her sister, Sophia." Ashley threw her arm around Sophia's shoulder.

"I think she's beautiful like her mother. Look at those dimples." Ashley smiled and flashed a set that matched her daughter's.

"Marrying your father was both the worst thing and the best thing that ever happened to me."

"I totally get that," Lydia said. "Being kidnapped meant I ended up with Clint, and it was both the worst thing and the best thing." Ashley held out her fist, and Lydia bumped hers against it.

They got outside and saw the limo waiting in the street. In unison, they stared in disbelief.

"Your chariot awaits, ladies."

"You've got to be shitting me," Ashley said to Drake.

"What?" he said innocently. "Your driver got sick, and I volunteered to take his place."

Sophia stifled a giggle as she saw Ashley's outraged face.

"This is totally unacceptable." She pulled her cell phone out of her tiny little purse and started to dial. Drake walked over and casually pulled the phone out of her hands.

"Hey, you can't do that."

"I just did."

"Seriously Drake, this is Sophia's bachelorette party, and you are not going to wet blanket it."

"I'm not, I promise. Hell, I'm going to help you up on to the bar top if you want to dance there. I swear. I'm just going to make sure nobody takes advantage of four beautiful women."

"I can take care of them. I'm taking them to safe places. I'm not stupid."

"Nobody said you were stupid, but men are going to be crawling out of the woodwork when they get a load of the four of you. Did you do makeovers?" Sophia felt her cheeks heating as Drake took in her outfit. She watched as Beth took a step behind Lydia.

"Drake, are you making snide comments about how we look?" Lydia walked up to the man and shoved her finger into his chest.

"Fuck no, are you kidding? Lydia, Beth, and Sophia look hawt." He turned to Ashley. "You're a fucking menace. These three have always looked great, but you've turned up the dial to ten. If I were to take pictures of them right now, their men would be here so fast it would make y'alls head spin." Ashley buffed her fingernails against the thin material of her blouse.

"I did good."

"Too good. Which is why I'm here."

"Jack sent you? He was worried about what I'd do?" Sophia loved seeing Beth start to build up a head of steam. It didn't happen often but when it did it was a beautiful thing. "I've never given that man one damn thing to worry about."

Drake held up his hands and backed up a step. "Whoa. This is totally my idea. Mason was worried so I–"

"Mason was worried?!" Sophia took up where Beth left off. "How dare he? I'm with Beth, I've never given him any reason to think I'd do anything to betray him." She struggled with the tiny purse Ashley had given her so she could call Mason.

A shrill whistle rang out.

"Ladies, your men totally know you're one hundred percent faithful to them. They worry about your safety. They think Ashley is a little bit crazy." Sophia stopped fumbling with the purse. She had to agree with that assessment, Ashley was a little bit out there.

"They have no idea I'm here right now. This was all my idea, and it was a brilliant one." Lydia snorted, and Beth giggled. "Now get your beautiful tushies into the limo and allow me to chauffeur and protect you around town." He opened the door for them. "Where are we headed?"

"The Gaslamp Quarter," Ashley promptly responded.

"Figures. You know the limo won't work down there, we'll have to park and walk." Drake griped.

"Oh, is it too much for the big bad SEAL?"

"Again, get your butts in the car. I like walking."

"Drake, you're one of a kind," Ashley said kissing his cheek as she got into the back of the vehicle.

Served him right, Sophia thought as she sipped

the pineapple flavored martini. Drake had promised to support them in their endeavors, and Ashley decided to take him up on it. The girl was literally dancing on top of the bar. How she'd known about this place, Sophia didn't know. They'd left the relative safety of downtown San Diego and were now in a less well-known area.

She took another sip of her drink.

"I think it was a twenty dollar bill!" Beth exclaimed. Sophia squinted and nodded. Yep, the man had actually thrown a twenty at Ashley as she danced. She wasn't the only one on the bar top, but she was the only one in a dress. All the rest of the girls were wearing jeans. Her panties were clearly visible. Thank God she wasn't wearing a thong.

Drake pulled another man away from the bar who tried to touch Ashley.

"Sophia, how many martinis have you had to drink?" Lydia asked.

"I don't know? They aren't really strong. Mostly pineapple juice," she yelled above the music.

Lydia pulled the drink out of her hand and took a sip. "You're cut off, girlfriend. I'm going to go get you a bottle of water. Beth, keep an eye on her."

Sophia watched as Drake pulled yet another man away from the bar. He had thrown a bunch of bills at Ashley. Ashley was making a shooing motion at Drake, who was beginning to look a little harassed. It was clear he was regretting his promise to support their antics tonight.

Sophia felt a man's hand sweep up her waist, and she let out a cry. Sophia tried to elbow the man but missed. She was feeling too muzzy headed. She saw Drake look up, and his face darkened. Drake started making his way over to them, but he was too far away.

"Asshole. Keep your hands to yourself." Beth's arm shot out, and Sophia heard a grunt behind her. Lydia was beside her sister in a heartbeat and had Sophia wrapped in her arms. Beth was now standing over a man.

"Get up, I dare you," Beth growled at the man.

"Bitch!" A redhead came up from behind Beth and pulled her hair. "That's my boyfriend!"

"Well, he should have kept his hands to himself." The woman swung wildly, and Beth ducked. The woman hit a man who was standing behind Beth.

"What?" He looked confused and turned to the man next to him and shoved him. Then all hell seemed to break loose. Sophia watched in awe as another man pushed against Beth, and Lydia grabbed him and threw him to the floor. But then she was elbowed, and her head jerked back.

"You bastard, you hit my sister," Beth cried. This time, Sophia was able to see the straight arm shot to the throat she must have performed on the man who had originally touched her. It was amazing and, this man too fell to the floor.

Lydia got a punch into his ribs on his way down. It was a beautiful sight to behold.

"Dammit! Cease and Desist! The next man or woman who comes next to these three dies!" Drake Avery roared. All movement close to them stopped. It was like they were in a little bubble of peace and quiet while mayhem surrounded them in the honky-tonk.

"What about Ashley?" Beth asked.

"Follow me." He pulled Sophia in front of him and had Lydia and Beth take hold of his shirt. Stay close." Every few feet he would stop and punch or elbow someone who got too close. Sophia saw one of the two Lydia's throw a punch as well. Maybe there had been alcohol in her pineapple juice since she kept seeing double.

Ashley was still dancing on the bar while the fighting was going on at floor level. Drake strode across the club like a hot knife through butter. Sophia heard the faint sounds of sirens.

Two men were trying to climb up on the bar. Drake set Sophia aside, grabbed both of them by the back of their necks, and sent them flying backward.

"Ashley Richmond, get down immediately." Ashley stopped mid-shimmy and assessed Drake.

Then she wound her arms over her head, cocked her hip, and twirled.

Drake was a tall man, he leaned over the bar, grabbed her around the back of her knees and had her over his shoulder in one smooth move.

"You bastard," she shrieked. Sophia looked at Beth and Lydia and knew she wore a similar expression of shocked amusement. Ashley had definitely met her match. They followed the two out of the bar, and the sirens got louder, it was definitely fun to watch Drake try to subdue the pretty blonde without doing damage.

"Ashley, the cops will be here any moment," Drake said desperately. "Would you quit acting like a spoiled three-year-old having a tantrum?" Ashley wiggled harder to get out of his arms.

"Quit manhandling me you big oaf."

"We're so going to jail." One of the two Lydia's yelled over the fighting.

They made it outside to the limo as the cops arrived. Drake poured Ashley inside the vehicle while Beth and Lydia helped Sophia in because it seemed like there were three doors.

Drake ran around to the driver's seat and whisked them away. Vaguely Sophia noticed they weren't headed towards Ashley's house. But mostly she was looking up through the moon roof and counting stars.

"Oh shit. I think he's taking us to Sophia's

house. We're so fucking busted," Lydia said.

"I'm not. Luckily I've had the good sense not to get involved with a SEAL." Ashley sat calmly re-applying her lipstick.

"Lydia, I think you might be getting a black eye," Beth said. That woke Sophia up out of her stupor. She peered at Lydia. Both of the Lydia's in her vision definitely had a swollen eye.

"Ya shad ice," Sophia said helpfully. All of the girls giggled.

"Are you feeling carsick?" Ashley asked.

"Nope. Feels floaty."

Lydia depressed a button and the glass that separated the driver from the passengers slid down.

"Drake, why are we headed to Sophia's house?"

"I've called your keepers."

"What?"

"Y'all need keepers, and I've called them. They're meeting us there. Ashley, I've called in some extras, so be fucking thankful. If I hadn't you'd be over my knee."

"As if."

"Exactly." The glass slid up.

Ashley pulled her mascara out of her purse and started applying it. "What did he mean by extras?

"Holy shit. I think we might have problems."

"I think you shouldn't do any of the talking," Lydia said. Beth slid her hand under her armpit.

"I think ya bose needs ice."

"You're right Lydia she can't talk," Beth agreed.

"What did Drake mean about extras?" Ashley asked again. The limo pulled to a stop. The door opened, and there was Mason. He looked worried.

"Come here, baby." He tugged at Sophia's hand, and she teetered as she got up to go over to him. He scooped her out of the car and carried her up the walkway into the house.

"I love it when you carry me."

"Fuck Lydia, you're hurt!"

"It's nothing." Sophia looked over Mason's shoulder, and she saw Clint carrying Lydia followed by Jack carrying Beth. In the rear, Drake had Ashley in a fireman's hold, but he had his suit coat over her so her butt was sufficiently covered.

"Are they all right?" Sophia looked up and saw Darius, the SEAL team medic, holding the front door of her home open. Mason sat on the couch with her in his lap.

"Dare, can you get some ice for Lydia?"

"Ah shit. Lydia, what happened?" Darius asked as he headed towards the kitchen. Sophia saw Finn standing next to the fireplace. He looked amused, at least until Drake walked up to him and handed Ashley to him.

"She's yours, buddy. If I have to deal with her anymore tonight...well, suffice it to say, it won't end well."

"Drake, face it. You're not used to dealing with a

female version of yourself," Ashley said as Finn set her beside him. "I bet when you were my age you probably danced on the bar tops or the male equivalent."

Finn laughed. "I think she might have you there."

"What do you mean at your age? I'm not that much older than you," Drake protested.

"You're so old you forgot what fun is."

A shrill whistle pierced the room, and Sophia groaned.

"Sorry, honey. Drake. Ashley. Cut it out. Drake, I want a report," Mason demanded.

"Somebody laid hands on Sophia. I was dealing with this one." Drake jerked his thumb towards Ashley. "She was dancing on top of the bar, so I was across the room. Sophia was with Beth at the time. Beth laid the guy out with a straight arm punch to the throat. It was the last thing I saw as I made my way over because the crowd was in my way."

"Beth?" Finn questioned.

"Beth?" Mason asked.

"Beth? Are you sure it wasn't Lydia?" Darius queried Drake.

"My hand hurts, Jack," Beth whispered to her fiancé.

"Let me see." Jack pulled Beth's hand out from under her purse where she had been hiding it. "Dammit Beth, you're supposed to use the heel of your hand. Dare, can you bring more ice." Jack kissed her knuckles.

"I've been taking self-defense classes," she explained to all of the amazed men.

"They're paying off, slugger." Drake laughed.

"I wan self daffy classes," Sophia said to Mason. Mason shook his head.

"How much did you have to drink, honey?" he asked, tilting her chin up so he could brush her hair away from her face.

"Jus some pine juice. Was soooo good."

"Pineapple martinis," Lydia explained.

"Don't think you're getting off the hook. How in the hell did you get a black eye?" Clint demanded.

"Trust me, between Beth and I, the guy is still on the floor," Lydia explained. She tried to straighten up in his lap, but he held her tight in his arms.

"Drake, what the hell were you even doing out with the girls tonight?" Clint asked. "I thought this was the bachelorette party."

"It was. And aren't you thankful I was there? Otherwise, your fiancés, Rocky, Beyoncé, and Miss Tipsy would all be in jail."

"I'm taking Rocky home."

"I'm taking my fiancé home and getting her a steak to put on this eye."

"A steak?" Lydia shuddered. "Why would I want to put meat on my eye?"

"It's an American custom."

"It's barbaric." Clint easily stood up with her still in his arms. Sophia smiled at the strength it took to do that. She loved knowing Mason could do it as well. Then she frowned, remembering his shoulder wound.

"Why the frown?" he whispered into her ear. "Are you hurt?"

"Nos, I'm fine."

"I'm taking Ashley home," Finn said. "I think you two need a time-out." Sophia watched as everyone left their home and soon it was quiet.

"Where's Billy?"

"He's over at Todd's house again. If he hadn't been, we would have done this at Clint's house." Sophia nodded. Mason stood up with her in his arms.

"Mason," she protested. "Yous shoulder."

"I'm putting you to bed. Then I'm bringing you two bottles of water and some aspirin, which I expect you to take and drink before going to sleep. Do you hear me?"

"Yes, lieutenant."

"Good girl."

Sophia nuzzled his neck. What was it about being called a good girl that got her motor running?

"Sleep for you."

"Yes, lieutenant."

5

"No."

"I need you."

Mason woke up, he heard the last few words spoken by Sophia. He didn't wake her up immediately. She hadn't had nightmares like this since her attack two years ago, and now this was the fourth or fifth time he had caught her thrashing around. He knew the reason for the dreams now. It was since he had come home wounded.

This time, she was talking in her sleep, and he wanted to hear what she had to say.

"Please. Please let me tell you. Please. No. Don't go. I love you." She started to cry. Oh God, she was imagining him dying. It was breaking his heart.

"Sophia, wake up. Honey. You're having a bad dream."

"Mason?"

"You had a bad dream. Can you tell me about it?"

Sophia shuddered. "Mason, can you just hold me," her voice broke.

"I am, baby."

"Tighter." He gathered her closer, pressing his cheek against her damp hair. For long moments, they stayed like that until finally she calmed.

"Can you tell me about the dream?"

"I really don't remember it. I just remember the feelings. I woke up feeling so sad like I was reaching for something I had lost. I've woken up a few times like that lately."

"You haven't lost anything, I'm here." She looked at him. In the moonlight, he could see her beautiful green eyes.

"I thank God for you every day. Do you know that, Mason? Do you really know that? I worry I don't tell you enough how much I love you and what a good man you are." Mason felt a lump forming in his throat.

"Sophia, even when you aren't saying the words you're telling me. Your love shines through."

"But it's not enough. I need to tell you."

"And you are." She snuggled closer, and he felt her breathing begin to change. She fell asleep in his arms. He wished sleep would come as easily for him. He scooched them down so they were resting on the pillows and she sighed in pleasure.

He mulled over everything that had gone on since he had been home. Sophia hadn't said anything about his injury, seeming to take it in stride, but it was obviously weighing heavy on her mind. His captain, Larry Osterman, had been talking to him about taking a position in command. He could help straighten out all of the fuck-ups with the intel. Mason immediately rejected the idea. He knew his real strength was in leading a team in the field. What's more, Osterman was kicking ass and taking names. Mason knew he would get things straightened out. Still... Was this something that would ease Sophia's mind?

Sophia cuddled closer, it was clear she wasn't going to have any more nightmares, but Mason wasn't going to get any sleep that night.

Sophia watched Billy plan for the 'bachelor party.' It was perfect. Every single day Mason made her fall in love with him a little bit more. Billy worried to death how to come up with something since he was the best man. He took his duties seriously, and he had been working on the toast for over a month. But the bachelor party had him tied in knots.

She'd mentioned it to Mason and the next thing she knew Billy had come back from Lacrosse practice with a plan. Finn Crandall was Billy's coach, and she knew he helped her brother come up with the plan. Billy, Mason, and all the groomsmen were going to go surfing and spend most of the night at the beach. It was perfect.

"Sophia, Finn told me all of the team were older now, and they were done with all of the partying. They aren't like Ashley."

Sophia winced.

"How'd you hear about Ashley?"

"For God's sake, as soon as I saw Lydia with a black eye she spilled the beans. Did Ashley really dance on top of the bar? Drake really let her do that?" Billy's eyes were wide as saucers. He might be taller than she was but he was only fourteen.

Sophia sighed. "Yes, she did."

"I would have given anything to be there. I wanted to make sure it was true before I told Todd."

"I'm begging you, please don't tell your friends. They'll see her around the house, and I really don't want them thinking bad about her."

"Are you kidding?! They'll think she is the coolest woman in the world," Billy enthused. He went to the fridge and pulled out the fixings for a sandwich. Sophia watched in amazement as he piled on enough meat to feed a small army. Or at least, a SEAL team.

"Why don't you make two sandwiches instead?"

"I'm watching my carb intake." Sophia shook her head.

"Seriously?"

"I don't want to get slow on the field. I'm saving all the carbs for the cookies you baked."

"There is something wrong about a teenage boy talking about his carb intake."

"Todd's a wrestler. At least, I'm not spitting in a towel to make weight." Sophia shuddered at the thought.

"Hey, can you drive me over to Mrs. Crandall's. She got Rebecca a PlayStation, and I want to teach her how to play Call of Duty."

"Sure."

"Hey, Billy there's something I wanted to talk to you about. I'm going to go over to Frannie and Tony's next week. They kept the two boxes of stuff from the trailer. There wasn't much left, but I think I'm finally ready to go through it. It's mostly Mom's stuff. Do you want to go with me?"

Billy looked up from his sandwich and came around the island and put his hands on her shoulders. She had to look up at him.

"If you need me to, sure, I'll go."

"Thanks. I think it's finally time."

MASON LOVED SURFING during the magic hours. According to artists, they were the first hour of light after sunrise and the last hour of light after sunset.

He agreed, there was something magical about them. The water sparkled, and he could swear the waves rose to meet him.

He got lost as he sailed over the water on his board. He felt like he was flying and he laughed out loud, the salt water spray getting into his mouth adding to the experience and his pleasure. Down he would go, tumbling into the surf, and that too was exhilarating as he pushed his way to the surface, finding his board and climbing on top. He would paddle to the next wave and start again.

As he thought to himself that this was his greatest joy, he stopped short and fell into the water. Sophia. Hands down, Sophia was his greatest joy. More than anything he wanted to make her happy.

She'd had another dream the night before, this one even worse than the one three nights after the bachelorette party. Again she'd said the same things. "Please don't go. I need to tell you I love you." The more he thought about it, the more it didn't make sense. She always told him she loved him. But still, what else could it mean, except she was scared he would die on a mission?

This time, the wave caught him off guard, and he went down. Served him right. He needed to pay attention. How often did he tell Billy that? It was time to go ashore.

"You okay?" Darius asked over the sound of the

water as he maneuvered his board close to his and they paddled towards the beach together.

"Sure," Mason answered, and Darius raised his eyebrow.

"Okay, not good."

"You do realize this is your bachelor party. This is what you wanted to do. You're kind of supposed to be having fun."

Mason continued to paddle in silence while Darius waited him out.

"It's Sophia." Darius stopped paddling and grabbed Mason's board.

"Hold up and hop up." Mason watched in resignation as his friend sat up on his board.

"Is this private, or can anyone join?" Drake asked. Mason shook his head.

"It's not private." He looked over his shoulder towards the shore and saw Clint, Jack, and Finn were with Billy.

"Okay, so what's got our groom's panties in a twist? Have you found out, Dare? You drew the short straw."

"God dammit." Mason rubbed the back of his neck and then stopped. He hated when he was obvious. And he knew when he did that it was obvious he was upset about something. The guys laughed.

"Spill it," Drake demanded.

"Ever since I came home wounded Sophia's

been having bad dreams. She hasn't done that since those two assholes attacked her a couple of years ago." Mason looked out towards the moonlit ocean hoping to find answers.

"Shit, that's to be expected."

"No, it's not. She's even lost some weight she couldn't afford to lose. This is really getting to her."

"So when you asked her about it, what did she say?" Darius asked.

Mason swirled his hand in the water.

"You haven't fucking asked her?" Drake shouted.

"Keep your voice down. I don't want Billy to hear."

"You haven't asked her? Are you dumb?"

"There's no point. I know what it is. She's scared I'm on the teams, and she doesn't want to tell me. She'd never tell me. She always puts her own needs last, and I'm not fucking having it."

His outburst was met with dead silence. Darius and Drake looked at one another.

"Aren't you going to ask me?"

"Don't have to," Darius said. "Have you made up your mind?"

"Pretty much. I'm going to talk to the captain after the wedding."

"You'd be working the intel?" Darius asked.

"Yeah, Osterman asked me to do it right after

our last goat fuck of a mission. We talked, and I turned him down after suggesting Marty."

"Marty would be great. You'd be better," Drake said. "This is fucked up. This is royally fucked up. You are the stupidest man on the planet. You need to talk to your woman."

"Nope. And you guys better plant some smiles on your God damn faces. Billy has been planning this party for weeks."

"And just when do you think we got stupid?" Drake asked.

"Sorry. This shit has me all twisted up."

Darius stopped Mason's board again. "Mase, you know whatever your decision is we have your back, right?"

Mason felt his chest tighten.

"Yeah. Even if you do abandon us," Drake said with a grin.

"You're an asshole, Avery," Darius said to Drake, shaking his head.

"It sounded like a Hallmark commercial. I couldn't help it."

Mason laughed at their antics.

HE SAT PROPPED up against a piece of driftwood and drank a Pacifico beer. He loved seeing Billy get so much attention from his team. Right now he was practically rolling in the sand with laughter. Dare was telling him about Drake's first time on a surfboard. It *had* been a sight to behold.

Drake being Drake had been sure it would be a piece of cake. The best part had been when he had come up after a tumble and proceeded to sit up on his board and face the shore. He hadn't seen the large wave that crashed down on top of him. Everyone on the shore had been clapping and cheering for him when he had finally come ashore. He finally started to listen to the experienced surfers after that.

"Billy, how are Jack's lessons going? Is he listening?"

"He's a great student."

"You're a great teacher. You've saved me from drowning the few times you've taken me out," Jack drawled.

"You've caught on really fast," Billy said enthusiastically.

"How's Lacrosse going? You doing okay, despite the fact your trainer sucks?" Drake teased.

"What are you–" Billy began belligerently before he realized Drake was teasing about Finn. Then Billy shot Finn a sideways glance. "I suppose I'm doing somewhat okay. I'm hoping I might get someone who can really teach me something next year."

Finn lunged for Billy, and Mason watched as

Billy got up and sprinted down the beach with Finn in pursuit. Billy was pretty damn fast.

"You're raising a good kid," Jack said.

"You really are," Darius agreed.

"He really is raising himself. Either that or Sophia is doing it." Drake broke out laughing.

"What?" Mason asked.

"You're the kid's idol. Hell, he's even taken on your mannerisms. Learn to take a compliment." Mason threw a piece of driftwood Drake easily dodged.

"I still think you need to talk to Sophia," Drake said.

"Our women are a lot tougher than you think." Mason wasn't surprised Darius and Drake had managed to fill in Clint and Finn. He turned to Clint.

"Sophia isn't Lydia. Lydia is the type to want to fight beside you, Sophia isn't."

"Beth is more like Sophia," Jack said, "wouldn't you agree?"

"Yes," Mason said carefully.

"She has a spine of steel same as Sophia. I think you're reading her wrong. You need to talk to her."

"Look, guys, I appreciate your counsel, I really do. But my mind's made up. I absolutely refuse to put Sophia in the position of the bad guy. It's clear what her nightmares and weight loss mean. My job is to protect her, to cherish her."

"This is going to kill you, Mase. You know you were meant to serve in the field. That's where your skillset is it's where your heart is." Clint gave him the same steady gaze as everyone around the bond fire.

"And you all know our time in the field is finite. Eventually, we'll all end up behind desks, I'm just taking the job sooner. I'll still have your backs."

"You're acting like a fucking dumbass," Drake's accent was thicker than normal meaning he was truly upset. Mason couldn't do anything about it.

6

SOPHIA WIPED HER SWEATY PALMS AGAINST THE ON
her jean-covered thighs.

Billy grabbed her hand. "It's going to be
all right."

"It'd be nice if something was," Sophia
mumbled. She couldn't sleep and most nights
Mason would come home and walk around the
house like he'd lost his best friend. But the few
times she tried to broach it with him, he'd tease her
about their upcoming wedding and ask her about
her red dress. Normally she'd have put her foot
down and demanded answers, but she was too
stressed about today.

"Sophia, why now? Why days before your
wedding? I don't understand?"

"I don't quite get it either, Billy."

Sophia fished the key to Frannie and Tony's

house out of her jean's pocket. They were over at the food bank, and Frannie had told her the boxes were in a back bedroom she used for storage. She had warned the Andersons they were probably going to have to hunt for them since they would be buried under other 'crap' as she put it.

"I asked her if she wanted to be here when we went to her house but she really didn't seem to care."

"Of course, she didn't, Soph. It isn't like we're going to jump on her beds." Sophia giggled.

"Jump on her beds? Where do you come up with this stuff?"

"It's why you love me." Billy bumped her shoulder as they entered the house.

The back bedroom was easy to find.

"She wasn't kidding about it being full of crap. How much stuff does one woman need?" Billy asked.

"Oh hush up and start looking. I marked all sides of the boxes, 'Anderson'."

"Thank God."

Billy made quick work of moving boxes. When Sophia went in to help, he immediately told her to stop.

"I've got this. Just keep your eyes peeled."

"Billy, I'm more than capable of lifting boxes."

"I didn't say you weren't. But I would feel better if you'd let me do this."

"You have been spending far too much time with Mason."

After ten minutes she saw the boxes.

"There they are. Behind the fake Christmas tree."

He was able to stack the two and maneuver his way to the door.

"Are you sure I can't carry one to the van?" Sophia asked.

Billy lifted an eyebrow in response. Yep, he had definitely spent too much time with those damn SEALs, she thought with a laugh.

They headed over to the food bank to drop off the key.

"Did you find everything all right?" Frannie asked.

When Sophia didn't immediately answer, Billy stepped in. "We found the boxes just fine."

"Sophia, are you going to be all right?"

"Yes," Sophia said automatically.

"Frannie, every time I ask Sophia why she's so upset about the boxes, she says it's nothing. But it's obviously something. What is it?"

"Billy!" Sophia looked at her brother, more than a little surprised at his blunt question.

"Well, I want to know. Frannie was with you a lot when Mom was so sick. I wasn't. I was with the Bards," Billy said, referring to his foster family. "Honey, you went to the funeral with your sister, I remember you being so little. I can't even fathom you being the same boy." Billy looked uncomfortable. "That asshole of a father didn't even come to your mom's funeral, do you remember?"

"Frannie, let's not rehash the past." Sophia put her arm around Billy's shoulder so they could go.

"The young man asked. Billy, do you remember how hard you were crying?" Sophia looked up at her brother, worried he would be upset, but Billy seemed to be looking inward trying to remember.

"I don't remember a lot about that day. Tell me more."

"You were about ten or eleven, and I swear if it were possible Sophia would have picked you up and held you in her arms. You were inconsolable. She never once cried, all of her attention was on you." Frannie turned to Sophia.

"All of your care had been on everyone else. Your mother and then on fighting to get Billy. When did you take the time to mourn?"

"I mourned every day. You of all people should have seen I was a basket case," Sophia protested.

"Are you out of your mind? You were a rock." Sophia gave a short laugh.

"I don't know who you saw, but I was barely coping."

"And coped, and coped, and coped. That's exactly what I'm talking about, girlie. You coped.

You never once took time for yourself. Billy, you asked me a question. You wanted to know why Sophia is so upset about these boxes. This might be her first real moment to mourn."

"I think you're both blowing this way out of proportion. Here's what really happened. Mason asked me why I didn't have anything from my past. No old pictures of me as a child. He was right, I should have unpacked these boxes two years ago. That's all. End of story." She stared the two of them down daring them to say anything else.

"Sorry, sis, I was just worried."

"Yeah, well don't," Sophia said.

Frannie frowned. "If you need me, you know where to find me." She hugged both of them and whispered something in Billy's ear.

"Are you mad at me?" Billy asked as they drove back to the house.

"Frustrated. Just frustrated. Seriously, Billy, I wished you would have taken me at my word."

"You never do when I say 'nothing.'" Sophia barked out a laugh.

"Okay, you win on that one. Look, I can't even remember most of the things in the boxes, and it breaks my heart. How can mom's life be distilled down to two boxes, and I can't even remember what's in them?"

"Don't you mean our life?" Shit, the kid, was too smart for his own good.

"Let's just get home."

BILLY HAD SET the boxes in the living room, but Sophia had insisted they have an early lunch before opening them up. She wanted to dig into them before Mason got home but part of her would be fine waiting until after Billy graduated from high school.

"Come on Sophia. I remember there being some cool pictures of us. I would love to have those up on the mantle."

He was right. She watched as he opened the first one. She had carefully wrapped everything in newspaper and then in tissue paper. She vaguely remembered doing that. Frannie had been right she hadn't cried once. What would have been the point? Mom was gone, and her sole focus had been figuring a way to get Billy out of foster care and to live with her. She hadn't had time for tears.

The first thing Billy unwrapped was a picture of their maternal grandparents at their wedding.

"Better check this out sis see if there is anything you need to do for your wedding." Billy let out a big laugh. Sophia grabbed the picture frame out of his hand.

"Hey, this is beautiful," she protested.

"You can barely see her she's so covered up. And

look at those suits. Mason is wearing his uniform right?" Sophia's heart skipped. The idea of seeing Mason in his dress whites took her breath away every time. "Earth to Sophia."

"Huh?"

"Never mind." Billy was taking the next couple of things out of the box and carefully opening them. They were obviously pictures. "This is the one of all of us at the Grand Canyon. I'm surprised Mom kept it."

"She kept everything with the two of us in it. It didn't matter if Dad was in the picture or not." Sophia traced her finger over her mom's face. She looked so vibrant in the photo. They got their smile from their mom. She took a deep breath.

"I think this box is nothing but pictures. Right?" Billy asked.

"Yep."

"Hey look, there are two photo albums."

"I completely forgot about those. Mom made those for us when she was getting sick at the end."

"How could you forget? That doesn't make any sense." Billy shot her an almost accusing glance.

"I never told you how bad it got, are you sure you want to know? I guess if you look at your album, you'll know." Sophia let out a sigh. "Mom's cancer went from her lungs to her brain. She had a lot of trouble remembering things. Doing things for herself." Fuck, she didn't want to tell Billy this, but he was already opening up the photo album that had his name on the front.

"Sophia, everything is crooked. It looks like a little kid put this together." She watched as he turned the pages.

"It was the best she could do, Billy."

"She put in every one of my class pictures, and they aren't even in order. Her handwriting is so hard to read. Words are misspelled."

As he turned another page, an envelope fluttered to the floor. It wasn't sealed, and it had his name written on it. Even that was hard to read.

"Soph?"

"I didn't know anything about this, Billy. If I had, I would have given it to you two years ago, I swear."

He opened it, there was one lined sheet of paper. The words didn't even manage to stay between the lines. Sophia read over Billy's shoulder. There wasn't much. Caroline Anderson was confused about the age of her son, that was clear, she wrote to him as if he were still in first or second grade.

She told him how much she loved him and how proud she was of him.

I wish I could have held you in my arms one last time. You and your sister were the two best things I ever did in my life. I know you'll grow up to be a man I'll be proud of. I wish I could be there to see you grow up. I want you to live a full and happy life. Find love, Billy. All the rest doesn't matter, as long as you are happy and find someone who you love and loves you.

"I wish I could have been there with you both. I wish they hadn't taken me away." Sophia was thankful they had, this way Billy had only good memories of their mother.

"How bad was it? How long did you have to deal with her like this, Soph?" he asked, pointing to the disorganized photo album.

"Not long."

"How long?" Billy wouldn't be put off.

"Probably three months."

He shoved his album aside and pulled her in for a hard hug. "Sophia, how did you manage to cope? She was so lucky to have you." Then he started to cry, and she held her brother, who really was still a boy no matter how big his body might have gotten. He was still only fourteen.

Finally, he calmed and gave an embarrassed laugh. "Let's open your album and see if you got a letter."

"Billy, is it okay if I read mine in private?" He gave her an assessing look and then hugged her.

"Sophia, whatever you need. What about the other box?"

"Can we get to it later? Maybe tomorrow, okay? I feel like baking."

"Want some help?"

"You'd still do that? I thought you were getting to old for baking with your sister."

"Not if I could get some chocolate chip cookies," Billy said with a grin. They got up off the floor. Billy picked up three different photos, two he put on the mantle and one he put on the side table beside a grouping of other pictures. Sophia left her photo album on the coffee table, excited at the prospect of baking with Billy. It had been a long time since he had wanted to do that with her.

7

"So I'm getting Anderson cookies and what else?" Mason asked as he came in the kitchen door.

"Sophia went all out. There's even banana cream pie and apple brown betty."

"So who's coming over for dinner?" Mason asked as he snatched some cookies off a plate and stroked Sophia's hair, then tipped her head up for a kiss.

"Nobody. I'm taking half of everything over to Jack and Beth's house. Jack wants another surfing lesson tomorrow morning, so they asked me to spend the night." Jack Preston hadn't pressured him the other night about Sophia, but he sure was clearing the decks so they could have some one-on-one time in case they *did* want to talk. The man was a sneaky bastard.

"Well I'm at least feeding you first," Sophia insisted.

"No, you're not. They promised pizza as long as I promised to bring dessert."

"Do you have any idea how much you eat?"

"Jack's even bigger than Mason. He's huge."

"He's got you on that one, honey. You might as well let it go." Mason gave Billy a fist pump.

"Oh, go get your stuff ready, I'll make sure the food is packed up. What time are they getting here?" The front doorbell rang.

"I guess that answers that question."

"All my stuff is ready to go and set out near the front door. Do you need help with the food?" Mason watched in awe as Sophia closed the last Tupperware container and put it into a shopping bag.

She handed it to Billy.

"Be good."

"Always." He looked between the two of them. "I'll see you tomorrow." They watched as he left through the front door.

"Three, two, one," Sophia said. They waited, and the door crashed open. Mason laughed.

"I forgot my phone," Billy said as he raced to his bedroom. Sophia and Mason walked out to the porch and waved at Jack, who was waiting in his SUV. Billy gave Sophia a quick hug and then jumped off the porch and was in the car before they could say goodbye again.

"I think this means we have the house to ourselves." There was a smudge of flour on Sophia's cheek. He loved when she'd been baking. Baking always made Sophia happy. "Let's get you inside, it's chilly."

"It's not chilly the weather's perfect."

"Okay, how about if I said we're too exposed for what I have planned for you, young lady?"

"I would say God Bless Jack and Beth."

"I would agree." He put his arm around her and guided her towards the kitchen. He perused the stove and oven and made sure everything was turned off before moving them down the hall.

"You mean we're not going to make out in the kitchen?" Sophia pouted.

Mason stopped and made to turn around, causing her to laugh. "Never mind, I think we need the flat surface the bed offers. I still have cookies cooling on the island. Otherwise, I might take you up on it, handsome."

"We've had some good times in that kitchen as I recall." He watched as she blushed. Despite being alone in the house, Mason still closed their bedroom door. It would be just like the kid to forget his damn wetsuit or some such shit.

Then Sophia took off her T-shirt and every thought flew out of his head, save one.

"My God, you are beautiful." She blushed again.

"Now you."

"Huh?"

"You take off your shirt." She walked up to him, and tugged at the hem of his black shirt, and he pulled it over his head. She kissed him in the middle of his chest, and he felt it down to his toes.

No matter what went on in her life, intimate time with Mason made everything else disappear. Her whole world tipped right side up and then narrowed so it was just the two of them encased in a bubble. She slid her arms around his lean waist loving the hard solid heat of his chest as it met her breasts.

"God, I've missed you," he murmured into her hair. She giggled.

"Hey, you aren't supposed to laugh at the man you're going to marry in four days."

"Mason, we just made love this morning. How could you have missed me already?" she asked reasonably.

He tilted her chin so blue eyes met green. "Didn't you miss me today?" He grinned down at her knowing the answer.

"I guess it's a good thing we're getting married."

She stood on her tip toes and nipped the dimple in his chin. Then groaned as he cupped the back of her head and kissed her. God, the man knew how to kiss. Slow kisses. Soft kisses. Melt your toes kisses. The list went on. Then she was lying on the bed naked.

He nibbled her jaw, and she sighed.

"Wife." He whispered. "That's my dream—to be able to call you wife." His hands played music down her body.

"My Mason." She could barely get the words out she was so choked up. "You're my Mason."

She tried to push him over wanting so much to make love to him. He shook his head. "Some other time," he promised. "Let me love you tonight."

"You always do."

"I need this, Sophia." Again she looked into his sapphire blue eyes and saw his truth and nodded.

His left hand cupped and molded her breast, his thumb teasing her until she begged for his mouth. He claimed her. She arched upwards. He was so much more forceful tonight, and she reveled in it. Sophia grabbed his hand and tried to move it towards her thighs. He easily clasped her wrists and placed her hands above her head.

"Keep them there," his voice was low and rumbly. She shivered and nodded. This was not the man she made love with that morning. He dipped his head and savored her other nipple like a long denied treat, at the same time parting her legs. He softly caressed her folds, and she could feel him smiling against her breast.

"Don't tease," she wailed.

He thrust two fingers inwards, and she moaned in satisfaction as he twisted and found just the right spot.

Sophia wanted to beg him not to stop, but words were beyond her. He must have read her mind because he continued, and then he brushed his thumb over her bursting clit, and she found a voice that only knew his name. "Mason," she cried over and over.

SOPHIA WOKE WITH A START. Dammit, it was the same dream. She wished she could remember it. Then she looked over at Mason and smiled. She stretched and winced. Then she smiled again. God, the man was a fantastic lover. If she were smart, she would marry him. She laughed to herself at her little joke. Then she got up, picked his shirt off the floor, and pulled it on as she walked to the kitchen to get some milk and cookies. She was hungry for what seemed like the first time in days.

She thought about her dream again. It was filled with regret, loss, and guilt. Maybe Frannie was right. Maybe she still hadn't dealt with the loss of her mom. The cookie suddenly tasted like sawdust as a wave of guilt hit her. It was the overwhelming sense she always woke with after her dreams, and she knew why. She set down the food and went out into the living room so she could look at the picture of Billy and their mom that Billy had set on the mantle.

That was when she saw the photo album her mom had made for her. She carefully picked it up and opened it. Her album must have been made first because it was much neater. Her mom had started with her birth certificate. Then there was a picture of her at her first communion. It wasn't until her middle school photos that things started to get crooked. As she got to the last page, she found the letter.

"Ah Mom, why didn't I know you had written me a letter?" Sophia felt like a piece of garbage that in those many months together in the tiny trailer, she hadn't realized all of the time and effort her mom had put into making these photo albums or the fact she had written these letters.

"I suck," she said. She blew hair out of her eyes and tried to hold back the threatening tears. She bit her lip and opened the envelope, it was dated two weeks before her mother died. It was hardly legible, but Sophia could read it.

SOPHIA,

No woman could be prouder than I am. You are the best daughter in the world. I know you are going to try to deny this, but I need you to listen. Really listen. Long before I got sick I thought you were wonderful but now I know how truly exceptional you are. You are such a kind and loving girl. You don't see yourself clearly, but I do, and all of us who have been gifted with your presence in our lives are truly blessed.

There hasn't been a day that has gone by that you haven't made me feel loved and cared for. Considering the fact you have had to care for me like I was a baby makes you a very special woman, Sophia. I love you more than words can say.

I know that even with my passing you are going to take on a monumental task of raising a young boy. I know Billy couldn't have a better person to raise him. But remember to love and care for my daughter. She deserves all of the good things life has to offer. She deserves love and happiness because that is all she has ever brought to anyone else in this world.

Find a man who will love and cherish you. I wish I could be there to see you shine on your wedding day, and to hold my grandchildren. I know you will be an extraordinary mother. Know that every day I will be watching over you from Heaven.

I love you,

Mom

"Oh Mom, I hope you're watching right now." Sophia re-read the letter three times and then curled up on the floor.

"I love you too, but you can't love me. You can't mean those things."

She knew how she had been at the end. Her mother had been a burden. Sophia had tried not to show it. She had tried to be good and loving and supportive. But sometimes it had all been just too overwhelming.

"I tried to be good. I tried, Mom, I tried." So many tears, she saw one spatter on the letter and sobbed harder trying to wipe it off. Not wanting anything to damage it. She put it back in the album.

She remembered that twice her mother had been sleeping, but still in pain, and she'd leave her there because she just needed space. Sophia knew she had been the worst daughter in the world.

"Ah God, Mom." She grabbed the second box still on the floor and yanked it open. She knew it had some of her mother's things. Not photos. She started pulling the contents out until she finally found what she was looking for. Her mother's jewelry box. She clawed at the tiny little clasp and finally got it open. All of the jewelry fell out in a jumble.

"Dammit! Look what I've done now." She pawed through the pile, but couldn't find what she was looking for. "I can't find it, Mom. Your locket I can't find it." More tears came.

She held up the tangled mess and sobbed.

"Why can't I do anything right? I'm sorry, Mom."

Big, strong arms swept her up and carried her to the sofa.

"Go way. Need Kleenex." Mason understood her slurred words. He kissed her forehead and was back before she even realized he had left. He had brought a glass of water for her too. He blotted her tears and then waited for her to blow her nose.

"Drink this." When her hands trembled, he held the glass steady for her as she sipped the water which only made more tears leak. His was just the kind of love her mom had been talking about.

"Can you tell me?"

She shook her head. He set down the glass of water, pulled her in, tucking her head under his chin, and held her close. She breathed in the scent of him. It soothed her.

"This is helping," she finally said.

"I'm glad."

She spied the letter where it lay on the coffee table. She reached for it and handed it to him.

"Before you read it, I need you to know some things, okay? And I need you to really look at me and listen. And not listen through the lens of someone who loves me. Can you make that promise? On your honor?"

"On my honor."

"In the end for the last two months of my mother's life, it was brutal. There were so many times she didn't recognize me. When she did, she was in so much pain the medication often didn't manage it. There were a few times we could reminisce about when she was all there. But they were few and far between." Sophia grabbed the glass and finished what was left of the water.

"Mostly it was bad. I hated seeing her like that. I was lucky to get two hours of sleep because she would talk and moan in her sleep. I would try to keep her spirits up, but sometimes I would just take off. That's how I ended up seeing you at Moonlight Beach. I should have been there with her. I actually lost my temper twice when she threw her dinner across the room. She thought I was poisoning her food."

"Oh Sophia, why didn't you tell me this before?"

"Let me finish."

"I yelled at my mother. I actually yelled at her. She was sick in bed, obviously sick out of her mind, and I yelled at her. What kind of monster was I? I didn't just do it once Mason, I did it twice. I swear to God, I don't know which one of us was sicker." Sophia took a breath, but it wouldn't come. She tried taking another, but nothing. She looked up at

Mason, and grabbed her chest, willing air into her lungs, but it was as if all the air had left the living room.

He sat them up and pushed her head between her knees.

"It's okay baby, you're having a panic attack." He stroked his hand down her spine, up and down. Up and down. She felt gentle kisses on the top of her head, as he whispered nonsense that made her smile. Finally, she felt air slip into her lungs.

He swung her around so she was once again nestled in his arms.

"Can I read the letter now?" She nodded. She watched his every expression. Watched as he rapidly blinked trying to stave off tears. Then he gave her that special Mason smile.

"Your mother was as special as you are. When did she write this, baby?"

"That's what I don't get. It was written two weeks before she died. It was after I was such a bitch." He sifted his fingers through her hair so he could cup the back of her head. "Oh, Mason. All that time with her and I don't know how she could have said such nice things. I hope she knew how much I loved her. I don't know how she could have when I was such a mess at the end."

"She knew, baby, she knew. Just reading this letter tells me she knew. Is that what the dreams have been about?"

"I hadn't been able to figure them out until now. She's been on my mind so much. Margie and Frannie have been great, but I wanted my mom to see me in my wedding dress." She grabbed the Kleenex box. "Fuck! When am I going to stop crying? It hurts so much. I want her back." Mason didn't say anything. He just held her.

MASON NEEDED to snag a tissue for himself. How could someone as loving and caring as Sophia think she had ever done anything she needed to atone for? He tried to imagine those last months in a tiny trailer with her mother, caring for her twenty-four-seven and *not* breaking.

She was sleeping soundly, he moved her so he could pick up some of the mess. He didn't want her to have to deal with it in the morning. He quietly and carefully placed all of the things back into the box, and finally picked up the jewelry, untangling it as he went. He made note of a bright silver locket he had seen Caroline wearing in each of the pictures around the house and set it aside. The rest he put back into the jewelry box.

He carried Sophia into their bedroom, happy with the way she snuggled up next to him. Tonight she would finally sleep without bad dreams. He hated the talk he was going to have to have with her in the morning. Not the one where he convinced her she had basically been sleep deprived and in a torturous environment, and, of course, she would have come unglued a couple of times, anyone would have.

He was also going to suggest she see the same counselor who had helped her after the attack she had suffered two years ago. But it was really her mother who had done the most healing thing possible by writing that letter. Caroline Anderson was one hell of a woman, and Mason was just sorry he had never had a chance to meet her. No, he wasn't worried about having that conversation at all.

It was the conversation where he had to tell Sophia he had been stupid and assumed instead of asking. She was going to kick his ever-loving ass from here to Coronado and back. Then the guys were going to take up where she left off. God, he really didn't want to have to admit to this, but two things were forcing him to come clean. One was Drake Avery. If he knew, eventually it would get back to Sophia. But the more important thing was he didn't want to keep something so important from the woman he was going to marry. He wanted to let her know how screwed up his thinking had been, and that he had learned his lesson. At least, he was pretty damn sure he had learned his lesson. Fuck, he *better* have learned his lesson.

"Mason?" Sophia yawned softly. "You're thinking too hard. Hold me and sleep with me." He smiled and kissed her swollen lips.

"You're right." He shifted down on the pillows, pulled her closer, and let his eyes drift shut. Just four, scratch that, three more days, and she would be his forever.

8

"Breakfast in bed? I must have really scared the hell out of you last night," she said in a teasing tone.

"You did," Mason said as he set the tray on her lap and fluffed one of his pillows behind her head. "More than that, you made me ache for you. Now eat up, then we'll talk."

Sophia looked down and saw he'd made her French toast, and he'd picked a lily out of their yard and put it in a vase. The man was always making her feel special. "There's too much food you're going to have to share."

He grinned.

"I think you planned that."

"Maybe." His smile got bigger. Then she noticed the second fork and she laughed.

"You're a good cook, Gault," she complimented.

"Thanks." He set down his fork.

"I'm not done," Sophia protested as he took her fork out of her hand.

"You stopped eating five minutes ago. You just want to avoid talking," he said as he took the tray off her lap and set it on their dresser. He came back and bracketed her with his arms and looked into her eyes.

"You were a good daughter. Your mother told you so."

Sophia let out a sigh. "I feel better knowing she thought so. But–"

"But what." Mason tucked a lock of hair behind her ear.

"But I still don't feel it in my heart. I should have done better."

"Can you do me a favor?"

"What?" she asked cautiously.

"Close your eyes." He waited until she did.

"Can you imagine yourself sick? Out of your mind with pain?" She grabbed his hands, hard. "Day in and day out the pain gets worse, and you can't take care of yourself. The only person you have to depend on is Billy." Sophia gasped. She could see it so clearly.

"Tell me. Tell me what you see," Mason asked.

"Poor Billy. He hurts so much. I see him so sad such suffering."

"You mean you?"

"No, Billy. I ache for him. He hates to see me like this. I feel so bad for him."

"But what about you?" Mason persisted.

"I don't care. I so appreciate him, and I hate to see him so sad."

"But aren't you mad when he yells at you?"

"Of course not! This is too much to ask," Sophia said vehemently. Her eyes popped open. She met Mason's soft gaze which was filled with understanding.

"You were in one of the worst situations imaginable. That's why they arrange for people to have days off, relief workers who can come in and take over for a while so the primary caregivers can take a break."

"I still took breaks when I shouldn't have, and I still lost my temper."

"Sophia, this guilt has been with you a long time. I think you might need some help seeing things clearly. Remember when you were having trouble after the attack?"

"You think I need counseling for this?" Sophia thought about the woman who had helped her before. She'd had a great deal of insight and Sophia had felt really comfortable talking to her.

"Maybe you're right, Mason. I can't seem to get over this by myself. But God, you helped so much. Pretending this was Billy and I really helped."

"I'm glad. There is something else that might

make you feel better. You have the opportunity to kick my ass for being a dumb shit." She tilted her head.

"Seriously, Soph, I fucked up. I assumed."

"I thought we've covered this before." She stroked his arm. He seemed to be feeling real badly.

"Just know I was trying to protect you."

"Dammit, Mason." She pushed up from the pillows. "I thought we got past that too. I'm a big girl. If I need your protection, I'll ask for it."

"You've got to admit, you've been twisted up lately. You've been having nightmares, and you haven't been eating. It all happened when I came back from the last mission with my shoulder wound."

"Yeah, because of this unresolved stuff with Mom."

"I know that now."

"Okay, so you assumed it was about your injury. It's not a big deal, but something sure as hell is. Spill it."

"I decided to take a desk job." She shoved at his chest. He didn't budge it was like pushing at a wall which just made her angrier.

"You decided to take a fucking desk job. Without talking to me? All because you thought I was upset? Mason, I can't believe this. You love leading your team. When did you make this decision? Have you talked to Osterman? Have you talked to your team? Am I the last one to know?" She kicked out from under the covers and stood up so she could stand over him. He bowed his head.

"No, yes, and no."

"God dammit!" She spun around and slapped her hand against the wall. Then she turned back so she stood over him again. "I'm so mad at you. Even if I was scared about your job, it was for us to talk over. This wasn't something for you to make a unilateral decision."

"Sophia, you know you would never ask me to stop leading the team even if it was tearing you apart. You'd just waste away."

"You're not giving me credit for being an adult."

"Yes, I am. I'm giving you credit for being the most caring and loving and compassionate woman I have ever met."

"Apparently a compassionate airhead," she growled.

"I'm so sorry. What can I say? I fucked up. It was an epic fuck up, and I have learned my lesson." Mason was still on the bed, looking at her, wearing his heart on his sleeve.

"Do you know how important this is to me? Can you understand this Mason? I have to trust you to be honest with me. I can't go into a marriage with someone who doesn't think I'm an equal." She turned away, and he reached out and gently grabbed her around her waist.

"Please, baby. You're not just my equal you're my everything. I would be lost without you."

Sophia stood still.

"I sometimes forget just because you are so loving, underneath you're the one who has kept your family together. You're the strong one. But please know it's a knee-jerk reaction for me to protect everyone not just you." She thought about him with his team and realized it was his nature, and she turned in his arms.

"Mason, this is serious. You can't do this again."

"I promise, I won't. I will talk to you about all things that impact our family."

"On your honor?"

"On my honor."

"I'm mad at you, but I love you. That hasn't changed."

"Thank fuck. So the wedding's still on?" he asked.

"Please tell me you didn't just assume we weren't getting married because of a fight."

"I immediately clarified, I get points for that, don't I?"

"Yes, Mason, you get points for that." She sighed.

THANK GOD FOR LINNIE GAULT. Sophia looked

around the hotel suite, and it could easily have been pandemonium. Instead, her soon-to-be mother-in-law had everything running smoothly. All of the bridesmaids were dressed, and Ashley was supervising the two women who were doing their hair and make-up. Sophia had protested at the expense, but Ashley had insisted this was her wedding present.

Every one of the women looked like a model. They were getting pictures of one another. All but Sophia. She was still in a robe. Linnie had insisted she be the last one dressed. She was confused because her dress was the most complicated to put on, but she trusted the woman. She definitely had been right about everything else.

"Are you doing all right?" Frannie asked.

"I'm perfect. I couldn't be happier." Frannie grinned.

"I never understood women being nervous on their wedding day. I was so excited to marry my Tony. I figured it would be the same for you. Today is going to be perfect."

Sophia smiled. It would have been perfect if her mom could have been there, but she remembered what she said in the letter, and she tried to keep that in her heart.

"Sophia, I have your something new for you." Lydia handed her a box. She let out a loud laugh. Inside was a garter that said 'Hooyah.'

"Oh my God! This is wonderful. I love it."

"Not as much as Mason will," Beth said.

"Here's your blue." Margie gave the hairstylist blue pearl pins that she placed in her hair.

"Can I give you the something borrowed?" Rebecca asked shyly.

"I would be honored."

Rebecca took off her charm bracelet and put it on Sophia's wrist. "Billy gave this to me. The apple is because I taught him algebra."

Sophia hugged the young girl.

"Thank you."

"Now she needs something old," Margie said.

"Yes, she does." Linnie looked around the room. "You'll have to go into the sitting room for a bit. Sophia needs some privacy."

"I do?"

"You do, sweetheart."

Everyone filed out of the room. Linnie was last. She gave Sophia a warm hug. "I'll be back to help you into your gown as soon as you're done."

"I don't understand."

"You will."

The door closed. Sophia went over to the window. She could see the gazebo where they were going to say their vows. She still teared up at the thought of Tony DeLuca giving her away. He had asked for the honor after Frannie had told him

Sophia wouldn't be inviting her father to the wedding.

The air shifted and she knew Mason was behind her.

She turned and gasped. He was resplendent in his dress whites.

"Isn't this bad luck?" she whispered.

"No, you're not in your dress yet Mom made sure."

"Why are you here?"

"I have your something old. Turn around."

She watched as he carefully placed a familiar locket around her neck. Her vision blurred. He stroked her nape as he hooked the clasp. He came around to stand in front of her, she was holding the heart in her trembling hand.

"How'd you know?"

"I found it from the jewelry box when I cleaned up that night." He traced her jaw. "Are you going to be okay?"

"I can't get it open."

"Let me help." He flipped the latch.

"Oh my God, it has another plate. It used to only have pictures of Billy and me, now it has another plate with Mom's picture too. How'd you do that?" She looked up at her own special miracle worker.

"I wanted you to have your mother here at your wedding, so I went and had a jeweler install another section with her picture." Sophia launched herself into his waiting arms.

"Every day I fall more in love with you."

"Ahhh, Sophia, that's only fair. Every single day you bring more joy into my life than one man deserves."

A knock sounded and after a long pause Linnie Gault peeked in. "Time to get this show on the road."

LINNIE MUST HAVE TOLD them about the locket because nobody asked about it. If they had, Sophia would have burst into tears. Instead, all of the women came back into the room and swarmed her like worker bees to the Queen.

"Sophia, this dress looks so much better in person. You look like a princess." Linnie wiped a tear away. Luckily it was a corset dress, so even though she'd lost a few pounds, they were able to adjust the dress. The white strapless gown shimmered against her golden skin. Finally, Linnie found her voice again.

"We have fifteen minutes people," Linnie said.

"That's bull, everyone knows they'll wait for the bride." Ashley quipped.

"We are not making my son wait for his bride." Linnie gave Sophia a wink.

"And I'm not waiting a minute longer than necessary to get married."

"You're just anxious for the honeymoon. I think it's awesome you've waited two years to consummate the marriage," Ashley teased.

"We are not talking about sex in front of the underage girls," Frannie said pointing to Rebecca and Louisa. Both girls were on the floor, Rebecca was trying to convince Louisa not to take off her shoes.

"Well, I'm off the market for a while." Ashley gave a dramatic sigh.

"Who's the lucky man?" Sophia hoped it wasn't Finn. She loved Ashley, but right now she wasn't someone she wanted any of Mason's teammates to get tangled up with.

"It is possible, just maybe, perhaps, someone kicked my ass and gave me a 'Come to Jesus Talk.'" Ashley pouted.

"Drake," Beth, Lydia and Sophia all said in unison.

"He was right. It's time I pulled my head out of my ass."

"Language," Linnie admonished.

"Pulled my head out of my derriere and acted like a twenty-seven-year-old mom. I needed to stop letting your dad's treatment rule my life."

"Ah sweetie, I'm so happy for you. It took me a

hell of a lot longer to come to that realization." Sophia gave Ashley a hug.

"Okay, it's time for you beautiful girls to line up. Louisa, are you ready to grab your basket?" Linnie asked.

"Easter Basket!" Louisa squealed.

Ashley knelt down in front of her daughter. "You get the chocolate after the wedding, remember? First, you have to throw the rose petals. Uncle Drake has chocolate waiting for you up front after your sister Sophia says her words."

"Okay. Chocolate." Louisa smiled at her mom.

Everyone headed out, with Linnie and Sophia bringing up the rear.

"I believe in angels, Sophia, and I know with all my heart your mother is looking down on you today."

Sophia grasped her locket.

"I feel like I have a piece of her here now because of Mason."

MASON HAD TOLD himself to commit everything to memory. This day was the most important of his life. He watched as every woman walked down the aisle, and they were gorgeous. First came Louisa, throwing petals like they were baseballs, causing everybody to laugh at her antics. Then Rebecca, a girl just beginning to blossom into womanhood, and then Margie, a woman who sparkled with excitement without a ruffle in sight. But just a small portion of his brain was occupied with those thoughts, the rest was focused on the French doors at the back of the hotel.

The wedding march started, and everybody stood up. Drake elbowed him, but he never even glanced his way. His eyes stayed steady on his prize. And there she was. It was like a punch to the gut.

"Steady," Drake whispered.

Mason blew out a long breath and tried to maintain his composure but not sure he could. *My God, she looks like a dream. My dream.*

He'd never seen anything close to her beauty. She was a vision flowing down the aisle towards him. One that would forever be etched in his memory. Her eyes caught his, and her smile was sheer radiance. Every other person fell away. It was just the two of them.

"Turn around," Drake whispered. It took a moment for the words to sink in. Mason had Sophia's cheek cupped, and she nuzzled closer. Her eyes opened, covered with a sheen of happy tears, and he bent to savor one last kiss before they joined in front of man and God. He caressed his hand down her tiny waist and gently turned her so they could be wed.

They shared their solemn vows, his voice heard

by the crowd. Her voice heard just by him and the Reverend. Then he was kissing her again, his head spinning as he finally, finally held his dream come true. His wife.

"My Mason. My Love. My Husband."

"I love you, Sophia Gault. You are my everything."

THE END

ABOUT THE AUTHOR

Caitlyn O'Leary is an avid reader and considers herself a fan first and an author second. She reads a wide variety of genres but finds herself going back to happily-ever-afters. Getting a chance to write, after years in corporate America, is a dream come true. She hopes her stories provide the kind of entertainment and escape she has found from some of her favorite authors.

As of winter 2018 she has fourteen books in her two best-selling Navy SEAL series; Midnight Delta and Black Dawn. What makes them special is their bond to one another, and the women they come to love.

She also writes a Paranormal series called the Found. It's been called a Military / Sci-Fi / Action-Adventure thrill ride. The characters have special abilities, that make them targets.

The books that launched her career, is a steamy and loving menage series called Fate Harbor. It focuses on a tight knit community in Fate Harbor Washington, who live, love and care for one another.

Her other two series are The Sisters and the Shadow Alliance. You will be seeing more for these series in 2018.

Keep up with Caitlyn O'Leary:

Facebook: tinyurl.com/nuhvey2
Twitter: @CaitlynOLearyNA
Pinterest: tinyurl.com/q36uohc
Goodreads: tinyurl.com/nqy66h7
Website: www.caitlynoleary.com
Email: caitlyn@caitlynoleary.com
Newsletter: http://bit.ly/1WIhRup
Instagram: http://bit.ly/29WaNIh

ALSO BY CAITLYN O'LEARY

The Midnight Delta Series

Her Vigilant Seal (Book #1)

Her Loyal Seal (Book #2)

Her Adoring Seal (Book #3)

Seal with a Kiss (Book #4)

Her Daring Seal (Book #5)

Her Fierce Seal (Book #6)

A Seals Vigilant Heart (Book #7)

Her Dominant Seal (Book #8)

Her Relentless Seal (Book #9)

Her Treasured Seal (Book #10)

The Found Series

Revealed (Book #1)

Forsaken (Book #2)

Healed (Book #3)

Shadows Alliance Series

Declan

Fate Harbor Series

Trusting Chance (Book #1)

Protecting Olivia (Book #2)

Claiming Kara (Book #3)

Isabella's Submission (Book #4)

Cherishing Brianna (Book #5)

Black Dawn Series

Her Steadfast Hero (Book #1)

Her Devoted Hero (Book #2)

Her Passionate Hero (Book #3)

Her Wicked Hero (Book #4)

Printed in Great Britain
by Amazon